For Louisa and Ada

THE MOON KEEPER.
Copyright 2020 by Zosienka.
Published by arrangement with
Debbie Bibo Agency. All rights reserved.
Manufactured in China. No part of this book may
be used or reproduced in any manner whatsoever
without written permission except in the case of brief
quotations embodied in critical articles and reviews.
For information address HarperCollins Children's Books,
a division of HarperCollins Publishers, 195 Broadway,
New York, NY 10007. ISBN 978-0-06-295952-2.
The artist used gouache paints and color pencils
to create the illustrations for this book.
www.harpercollinschildrens.com. Designed
by Alice Nussbaum and Amy Ryan.
19 20 21 22 23 SCP
10 9 8 7 6 5 4 3 2 1 ❖
FIRST EDITION

The Moon Keeper

words and pictures by

ZOSIENKA

HARPER

An Imprint of HarperCollinsPublishers

There is a letter addressed to Emile.
He's been invited to attend the meeting
of the night creatures to hear a very
important announcement.

The night creatures have chosen him
as the new moon keeper. Emile is honored,
because this is a very important job.

Emile prepares himself
for the task.

There are many things
he might need for
looking after the moon.

At dusk he climbs ninety-three steps
up the ladder to meet the moon.

Up in the sycamore tree,
Emile introduces himself.

The moon is beautiful and round.
Emile has never looked at the moon this way before,
and he realizes just how magnificent it is.

For several nights Emile
keeps watch over the moon.
He clears some obscuring clouds
and tells the fruit bats to move along
when they play too close.

Shoo oooo.......

There isn't a lot to do,
but Emile finds
the moon nice to talk
to in the stillness
of the night.

One evening he notices something strange.

Emile rubs his eyes. Is the moon getting smaller?

His neighbor nods
in agreement.
"Yes, indeed, it seems
to be shrinking."

The change is slight.
To be certain, Emile draws
a picture of the moon each night
and compares it to the one
from the night before. . . .

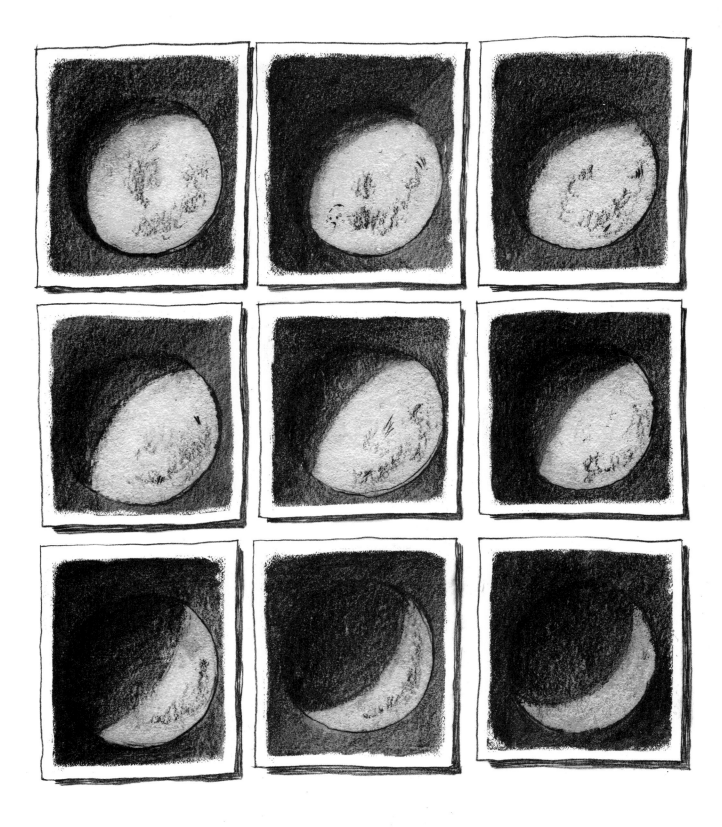

Emile hadn't imagined a
problem such as this. He rummages
through his tools and instruments,
but there is nothing there to protect
the moon from disappearing.

Think . . .
think . . .
think,
thinks Emile.

"Have you had enough
to eat, Moon?"

"Or are you sad?
Maybe the fireflies
can cheer you up
with a riddle,"
says Emile.

"Which fish only swims at night?"
asks a firefly.

"A starfish," replies another.

Emile giggles at the joke
and sees that the moon
is smiling too.

He phones his cousin in the jungle
to find out how the moon looks
over there.

It isn't good news.

"Same here, Emile,"
reports his cousin.

The moon grows thinner and thinner
until it's no thicker than a thread.

A big green bird lands beside Emile.
"I've lost the moon," Emile tells the bird.
"I was supposed to protect it, but I don't know
how to make it stay."

"Watch me," says the bird.

It jumps off the roof and flies into
the darkness. Emile stares into the night
trying to keep the bird in sight.

"I'm back," says a voice
behind Emile.

"Things come and go—you'll see," says the bird.

And then the moon blinks and vanishes.

The night is dark, but Emile pictures the moon in his mind
and repeats the words of the big green bird until he falls asleep.

When Emile wakes up,
there is a new smile in the sky.
"You're back," he whispers.

Each night the moon grows bigger and bigger, until . . .

. . . it fills the sky again.

31192021967912